**FRANCIS CLOSE HALL
LEARNING CENTRE**

College of
Cheltenham

D1485735

GLOUČESTER
College of Higher Education

Runes and Rhymes
and Tunes and Chimes

Runes and Rhymes and Tunes and Chimes

by

GEORGE BARKER

illustrated by

GEORGE ADAMSON

FRANCIS CLOSE HALL
LEARNING CENTRE
C & G C.H.E Swindon Road
Cheltenham GL50 4A
Tel: (01242) 532913

FABER AND FABER

London

First published in 1969
by Faber and Faber Limited
24 Russell Square London WC1
Printed in Great Britain by
Latimer Trend & Co Ltd Plymouth
All rights reserved

SBN 571 09122 9

College of St. Paul & St. Mary
Teaching Resources Library
The Park

874816

© George Barker 1969

To

Adam Alexander Rahere George Robert

This, Love, is what I say:
I see the swans on the river
when in the mornings of May
I look out of the window
at the break of day;
and I see them again
in the evening when
down goes the yellow sun.
I see them sleeping in their wings
as you do, my son.
This, Love is what I say:
I hope that you may
look out on the swans of morning
many and many a day
before you, and they,
lift up your wings, your beautiful wings,
and fly far away.

Contents

Contents

In foggy dawns

In foggy dawns
as cold as yawns,
in pitch black nights
when no moon lights
familiar sights
as she rides the rolling sky,
in kitchen, garden and in attic,
as though my pen was automatic
I make these rhymes
and tunes and chimes
for several children. Why?
Because my head
is like a bed
from which at times
these runes and rhymes
get up and start to fly.
They whiz about
both in and out
they make my room so cluttered
(as if I fell
down a wishing well

In foggy dawns

and all the wishes fluttered).
These runes and rhymes
and tunes and chimes
like gnomes and elves
disport themselves
on my bookshelves
in fours and eights
and tens and twelves
until I think that I'll
have neither chair,
chamber or stair
(and I've got many)
or table where
I can find any
room to spare,
for they'll be there
these rhymes like gnomes
these runes like elves
I make for children. I
think I shall run a mile.

2

How many apples grow on the tree?

How many apples grow on the tree?
    said Jenny.
O many many more than you can see!
    said Johnny.
Even more than a hundred and three?
    said Jenny.
Enough, said Johnny, for you and me
and all who eat apples from the tree
    said Johnny.

How many fish swim in the sea?
    said Jenny.
More than apples that grow on the tree
    said Johnny.
Even more than a thousand and three?
    said Jenny.
Enough, said Johnny, for you and me
and all who fish in the big blue sea
    said Johnny.

The Hamspringer jumps about in the bed

The Hamspringer jumps about in the bed
first on to my foot and then up to my head.
He squats like a grasshopper just by my nose
and twiddles a set of invisible toes.
Although he is small he is dressed like a king
with a robe and a crown and a thingmibob ring:
he appears in the most unpredictable places—
out of cracks in the wall or old pillowcases
or from under newspapers or out of the neat
little cave I can make in the top of the sheet.
I call him Hamspringer. Shall I tell you why?
He comes if I call it. That is why.

4

Should I ever again meet

Should I ever again meet
   the white horse that
I once saw in Harrogate
   wearing a straw hat,
well, if I wore mine then,
   (and I sometimes do)
I would raise it in the street
   as a matter of course
   in order to greet
   that Harrogate horse,
my friend, that be-hatted, sorrow-faced,
   Harrogate horse.

At midnight on the ice-bound Islands of the far-off Polar Seas

At midnight on the ice-bound Islands of the far-off Polar Seas
I have seen the Penguins sitting with their infants on their knees
Lunching off a pair of kippers just as placid as you please.

Why? Because the Polar Region, where the snow falls by the ton,
Confuses all its native creatures, Bear and Penguin, every one—
Remember that the Polar Region is the Land of the Midnight
    Sun!

Of evening in the wintertime

Of evening in the Wintertime
    I hear the cows go home
Mooing and lowing by the window
    in the muddy loam.

In other places other children
    look up and find no stars:
they see tall walls and only hear
    buses and motor cars.

I love the muddy lane that lies
    beside our lonely house.
In bed I hear all that goes by—
    even the smallest mouse.

The Dobermann dog,
O the Dobermann dog

The Dobermann dog, O the Dobermann dog,
O why did they buy me the Dobermann dog?
He is bigger than I am
by more than a half
and so clumsy at play
it would make a cat laugh—
he sprawls and he falls
over tables and chairs
and goes over his nose when he
stalks down the stairs.
He's the colour of seedcake
mixed with old tar
and he never knows rightly
where his feet are—
he growls in a fashion
to bully all Britain
but it doesn't so much as
frighten my kitten.
On the table at teatime

The Dobermann dog, O the Dobermann dog

he rests his big jaw
and rolls his gentle eyes
for one crumb more.
How often he tumbles me
on the green lawn
then he licks me and stands
looking rather forlorn
like a cockadoo waiting the
sun in the morn.
I call him my Dobe
O my Dobermann dog
my Obermann Dobermann
yes, my Octobermann
Obermann Dobermann Dog.

Never, my love and dearest

Never, my love and dearest,
    we'll hear the lilies grow
or, silent and dancing,
    the fall of the winter snow,
or the great clouds of Summer
    as on their way they go.

Never, my love and dearest,
    we'll hear the bluebells chime
or the whole world turn over
    after the starlit time.
O not everything, my dearest,
    needs to be said in rhyme!

Dibby Dubby Dhu rose one midnight

Dibby Dubby Dhu rose one midnight
   to sail his boat in the sky.
He knows that the stars are fishes
   and he even knows why.

Ask: "Why are the stars fishes?"
   Ask Old Dibby Dubby Dhu.
He'll answer: "Because they are silver
   and swim about in the blue."

I have seen him standing on tiptoe
   high on the tallest spire
and even on top of the weathercock
   to help him get up higher.

His long fishing line falls UPWARD
   instead of falling down
And he sees the North Star twinkling far
   below him in the town.

Dibby Dubby Dhu rose one midnight

His old fishing boat is anchored fast
    to the very tallest tree.
It bobs and rocks among clouds and church clocks
    as though the sky was sea.

He fishes for stars and birds. And once
    he almost caught the moon,
but his fishing line broke and, alas, he awoke
    just one moment too soon.

The tides to me, the tides to me

The tides to me, the tides to me
    come dancing up the sand:
when the waves break I lean to take
    each one by the hand.

The tides from me, the tides from me
    roll backward down the shore.
I do not mind, for I shall find
    a thousand and one more.

The Hi-Lo Snapdragoness
snorts fire

The Hi-Lo Snapdragoness snorts fire
as she curls by the Woomerong tree.
The flames fly out
from her angular snout
and scorch the Woomerong tree.

The Hi-Lo Snapdragoness snorts fire

At night from afar the Snapdragoness
can be seen with the naked eye;
    and you'd think from the smoking
    every chimney was choking
'twixt Woomerong and the sky.

High and low the Snapdragoness then roams
over the cloud-covered plain
    for a place far or near
    where the air is clear
and she can start breathing again.

Whenever I watch the

Whenever I watch the
  cows and sheep
cropping the grasses
  green and deep
on a summer day when
  all the trees sleep
and I see the big wheels
  turn and sweep
around the corn as
  they mow and reap,
then, then I wish
  that I could keep
watching the cows and
  the cropping sheep
and the men in the field as
  they mow and reap—
I wish I could watch them
  till I sleep
and then in dreams
  when the shadows creep

Whenever I watch the

    see dreaming cows and
      dreaming sheep
  and men who dream
    as they mow and reap.

Long ago, long ago

Long ago, long ago
when mountains were lumps
no larger than moderate
marzipan lumps
when the sea was no wider
than any duck pond
and you could see to China
and beyond,
when trees were no bigger than
twigs in the ground
and the world was as small
as a ball
and as round,
I wonder, rather,
yes, I wonder how
my great grandfather
and great grandmother
ever, ever found
enough room on the ground
to walk together
without falling off

Long ago, long ago

into nothing whatever,
yes, without falling off
into nothing whatever.

This is a rune I have heard a tree say

This is a rune I have heard a tree say:
"Love me. I cannot run away."

This is a rune I have heard a lark cry:
"So high! But I cannot reach the sky."

This is a rune I have heard a dog bark:
"I see what is not even there in the dark."

This is a rune I have heard a fish weep:
"I am trying to find you when I leap."

This is a rune I have heard a cat miaow:
"I died eight times so be kind to me now."

This is a rune I have heard a man say:
"Hold your head up and you see far away."

Dibby Dubby Dhu, Dibby Dubby Dhu

Dibby Dubby Dhu, Dibby Dubby Dhu,
    are you an Emperor?
And if you are not, why do such a lot
    of people think that you are?

"I walk with the step of a seven-foot king
    and if ever I took a wife
she'd be the best Queen that was ever seen
    in any Emperor's life."

Dibby Dubby Dhu, Dibby Dubby Dhu,
    are you a Professor at College?
And if you are not, why have you got
    so much extraordinary knowledge?

"I am as wise as an Ostrich Egg
    with nothing inside it but brain.
The wisest Professor is very much lesser.
    You see, I never explain."

Dibby Dubby Dhu, Dibby Dubby Dhu

Dibby Dubby Dhu, Dibby Dubby Dhu,
    Are you in fact a Magician?
And if you are not, why do such a lot
    of people think that your position?

"My position is vertical, and I stand here
    tatterdemalion and tragic.
Well, not tragic, my lad. Perhaps a bit sad.
    Why?—No one will pay for my magic."

Dibby Dubby Dhu, Dibby Dubby Dhu,
    then how can you be a King?
Since you have not so much as got
    one jot of anything?

"I am a King because whatever I touch,
    whatever I touch with my hand,
Gets up on its own, though it's stock or it's stone,
    and dances along the sand."

"This is why I am an Emperor,"
    said Dibby Dubby Dhu.
"If my hand was laid on your head you'd be made
    a king with a crown, too."

Where are you boats and roses

Where are you boats and roses
    I saw in the summertime,
Where are you now the year closes
    and it is wintertime?

Where are you swifts and swallows
    who flashed among the leaves
Where are you oak tree shadows
    and you yellow corn sheaves?

Where are you boats and roses

O where are the summer swimmers
 who sang when the sun shone?
The memory of you glimmers
 one moment, and is gone.

O child, child of misfortune

O child, child of misfortune,
    never sit there and weep.
The time comes when night and the bright stars
    fold up all sorrow in sleep.

When the angel of day arises
    from the marvellous fountains of dawn
See! at her breast lies smiling
    the child of misfortune reborn.

You many big ships with your billowing sails

You many big ships with your billowing sails
 gliding out on the seas of the morning
with bright flags flying and the sailors crying
and the wild winds blowing and the wild seas flowing
 and above you the Bird of Dawning:

To France and Spain and the Spanish Main
 and the Isles of Australia turning
your golden bows as the gale allows
when the green wave slides along your sides
 and you lean as though you were yearning

For some far shore where there's no more
 cloud or sorrow or weeping:
you flaunt your great sails through the storms and the gales
and in the calm night ride on the bright
 stars as though you were sleeping:

You many big ships with your billowing sails

Ships proud and splendid, it is never ended
    your voyage into the morning.
Though in storms and rains and wild hurricanes
you welter and wallow, you will still follow
    the beautiful Bird of Dawning.

Three Mandarins

Three Mandarins
of Cochin-China
(dressed up like peacocks
only finer)
sat sipping tea
in Carolina.

The first one said:
"I do not know
why I am here.
I think I'll go
back to the places
that I know."

The second said:
"The tea in China
is better than tea
in Carolina.
It is both more refined
and finer."

Three Mandarins

The third one said:
"A Mandarin
should like the places
he is in.
Even (Heaven help us)
Carolina."

On a quay by the sea

On a quay by the sea
with one hand on his knee
sat Skipper ("Double D.") Dhu,
resting his eyes on
the far horizon
for want of something to do.

Up and up like a cup
that can sip its own sup
rose the tides of the turbulent sea,
but gravely he sat
gazing over, not at,
the monsters that gnashed at his knee.

The whales lashed their tails
like terrible flails
and the shark clashed its portcullis jaw;
round and round by the jetty
like a lot of spaghetti
the octopus rose with a roar.

On a quay by the sea

Dhu sits and he knits
his brows as befits
a Captain among such a welter;
then he lowers his eye
and all of them fly
down to Davy Jones' locker for shelter.

The West is where the fiery Sun

The West is where the fiery Sun
    goes down into the sea,
and yet it rises the next day
    as bright as it could be.

This is remarkable, because
    like others, I was taught a
lesson that ran: "No fire can
    survive a dip in water."

Fishes wonder by the ferries

Fishes wonder by the ferries
 why the people go
back and forth from bank to bank
 daily to and fro
like a swing in the Park with
 nowhere to go.

Why do they come back again
 if they wish to get
to the other side without
 finding their feet wet?
I and the fishes have not heard
 a sensible answer yet.

I stood beside the big fish pool

I stood beside the big fish pool
   in the Flamingo Zoo
gazing at the still, still water
   so still, and so green, too.

I stood there in a day-dream, and
   no cloud or bird in the sky
Moved. All stood there stock, stock still,
   the pool, the noon, and I.

O! then the water, the still green water
   burst like a flashing gun
and mountain of dolphin leapt up out
   to bite the sky or sun!

It hung up in the noonday air
   like a looping aeroplane—
it fixed me with a hungry eye
   and then dived back again!

I stood beside the big fish pool

I think it was his dinner time.
I think he fixed an eye
upon me in the knowledge that
boys taste better than sky.

O Lobengula!

O Lobengula!
Where are you?
O Lobengula!
You haunt me. Who
or what are you?
Are you the Mountain
where the Old King keeps
his dead Court around him
while for centuries
and centuries he sleeps?
Or are you the Never
Never Never land
where I could walk with
a queen on either hand
each trailing her silver gown in
the gold and silver sand?
O Lobengula,
what and where are you?
Are you that old, old
long lost and forgotten
Gaelic Harp of Gold

O Lobengula!

whom only Oberon
in his hand may hold
plucking out such melodies
and sad heroic memories
as make the heart grow cold,
those stories, those stories,
the saddest ever told.
O Lobengula
where shall I find
your green gold vales
with haunted lakes
in green dales confined?
What moon rises over
your blue misted hills
and makes the evening waterfall
glimmer as it spills?
O Lobengula
home to you some
night of enchantment
I know I shall come!

25

Mary-in-the-Garden

Mary-in-the-Garden
who are you talking to?
O Mother, it is my brother Peter
I am talking to.

Mary-in-the-Garden
who are you walking with?
O Mother, it is my brother Peter
I am walking with.

How can that be, my Mary?
O how can that ever be?
Your brother Peter is far, far away
over the widest sea.

Mother, the sea he is over
No ship ever sails,
no sun ever shines there
and no wind stirs the gales.

Mary-in-the-Garden

He sleeps in those far islands, Mother,
so far that no ship or
bird ever rested by
that dark and farewell shore.

O Mary-in-the-Garden
then how can he walk with you?
O Mary-in-the-Garden
how can he talk with you?

In the Garden, in the evening,
said Mary to her Mother,
he comes to me over that sea,
My Peter, my Brother.

What does the clock say?

What does the clock say?
Nothing at all.
It hangs all day
and night on the wall
with nothing to say
with nothing to tell
except sometimes
to ting a bell.
And yet it is strange
that the short and the tall
the large, the clever,
the great and the small
will do nothing whatever
nothing at all
without asking it,
the clock on the wall.

The duck that sits beside the pond

The duck that sits beside the pond
　　when it rains cats and dogs
Thinks to himself: "O why does it never
　　never rain newts and frogs?"

The duck that wishes that newts and frogs
　　sometimes fell out of the blue
is ignorant of the remarkable fact
　　that, sometimes, they do.

Who is Dibby Dubby Dhu?
Who is he?

Who is Dibby Dubby Dhu? Who is he?
    Is he visible to the eye?
If I met him one fine summer morning
    would I see him as he went by?

He may be the man with the mowing machine
    you saw at work in the park
with a battered old hat and a waistcoat that
    is not really up to the mark.

I ask you: Is he an Inspector
    who goes round examining things
with a little black book and the serious look
    that constant inspection brings?

No. Dibby is not an Inspector.
    Nor is he a District Nurse
although, my dear, like all Nurses he'll cycle
    through thunder and lightning, or worse.

Who is Dibby Dubby Dhu? Who is he?

Who is he, then? Who is Dibby?
    Who is Old Dibby Dubby Dhu?
Be careful for he might easily be
    the person who's talking to you.

(Myself, I think Dibby's an actor
    who loves nothing so much as surprises,
and for this reason, in and out of season
    he adopts multitudes of disguises.)

29

What on earth are you doing here, Marvellous Mouse

What on earth are you doing here, Marvellous Mouse,
    sitting beside the wall
with one crumb of cheese balanced on your small knees?
    Do you not think it might fall?

What on earth are you doing here, Marvellous Mouse

    I am sitting here balancing cheese on my knees
        answered the Marvellous Mouse
    In order to see if a new friend might be
        attracted, and come to my house.

    But if I sit here all, all the night long
        awaiting my unknown friend
    I know very well I'll succumb to the smell
        and eat it myself in the end.

This line is written by the very hand

This line is written by the very hand
   of Dibby Dubby Dhu.
It has signed papers, dispelled the vapours,
   and crowned a king or two.

Observe me well. I cast a spell
   (as you may sometimes see)
like the wind running over grass
   or lightning in a tree.

Mark what I say. For, night and day,
   I shall be marking you.
I am King of the Air, and everywhere
   I look for marvels to do.

The cheetah, my dearest, is known not to cheat

The cheetah, my dearest, is known not to cheat;
the Tiger possesses no tic;
The horse-fly, of course, was never a horse;
the lion will not tell a lie.

The cheetah, my dearest, is known not to cheat

The turkey, though perky, was never a Turk;
nor the monkey ever a monk;
the mandrel, though like one, was never a man,
but some men are like him, when drunk.

The springbok, dear thing, was not born in the Spring;
The walrus will not build a wall.
No badger is bad; no adder can add.
There is no truth in these things at all.

The Pericodoolah

The Pericodoolah
(a tropical bird)
knows every song
yes, word for word
that she has ever
seen or heard.
She sings *so* sweetly
and with such art;
she does not repeat
a little part
and then forget and
go back to the start
for she knows every single
word by heart.

But the curious thing
about this bird
is that no matter at all
what the word
or what the tune
of the beautiful song

The Pericodoolah

in her beautiful head
something else always
comes out instead
and all that she utters
loud and long
without ever getting
one syllable wrong
(and dancing a tropical
slightly flip-floppical
topical Hawaiian hula-hula)
is this one sad word:
"O Pericodoolah!"